To Be Read At Dusk

By Charles Dickens

Index Of Contents

TO BE READ AT DUSK

One, two, three, four, five. There were five of them.

Five couriers, sitting on a bench outside the convent on the summit of the Great St. Bernard in Switzerland, looking at the remote heights, stained by the setting sun as if a mighty quantity of red wine had been broached upon the mountain top, and had not yet had time to sink into the snow.

This is not my simile. It was made for the occasion by the stoutest courier, who was a German. None of the others took any more notice of it than they took of me, sitting on another bench on the other side of the convent door, smoking my cigar, like them, and - also like them - looking at the reddened snow, and at the lonely shed hard by, where the bodies of belated travellers, dug out of it, slowly wither away, knowing no corruption in that cold region.

The wine upon the mountain top soaked in as we looked; the mountain became white; the sky, a very dark blue; the wind rose; and the air turned piercing cold. The five couriers buttoned their rough coats. There being no safer man to imitate in all such proceedings than a courier, I buttoned mine.

The mountain in the sunset had stopped the five couriers in a conversation. It is a sublime sight, likely to stop conversation. The mountain being now out of the sunset, they resumed. Not that I had heard any part of their previous discourse; for indeed, I had not then broken away from the American gentleman, in the travellers' parlour of the convent, who, sitting with his face to the fire, had undertaken to realise to me the whole progress of events which had led to the accumulation by the Honourable Ananias Dodger of one of the largest acquisitions of dollars ever made in our country.

'My God!' said the Swiss courier, speaking in French, which I do not hold (as some authors appear to do) to be such an all-sufficient excuse for a naughty word, that I have only to write it in that language to make it innocent; 'if you talk of ghosts - '

'But I DON'T talk of ghosts,' said the German.

'Of what then?' asked the Swiss.

'If I knew of what then,' said the German, 'I should probably know a great deal more.'

It was a good answer, I thought, and it made me curious. So, I moved my position to that corner of my bench which was nearest to them, and leaning my back against the convent wall, heard perfectly, without appearing to attend.

'Thunder and lightning!' said the German, warming, 'when a certain man is coming to see you, unexpectedly; and, without his own knowledge, sends some invisible messenger, to put the idea of him into your head all day, what do you call that? When you walk along a crowded street - at Frankfort, Milan, London, Paris - and think that a passing stranger is like your friend Heinrich, and then that another passing stranger is like your friend Heinrich, and so begin to have a strange foreknowledge that presently you'll meet your friend Heinrich - which you do, though you believed him at Trieste - what do you call THAT?'

'It's not uncommon, either,' murmured the Swiss and the other three.

'Uncommon!' said the German. 'It's as common as cherries in the Black Forest. It's as common as maccaroni at Naples. And Naples reminds me! When the old Marchesa Senzanima shrieks at a card-party on the Chiaja - as I heard and saw her, for it happened in a Bavarian family of mine, and I was overlooking the service that evening - I say, when the old Marchesa starts up at the card-table, white through her rouge, and cries, "My sister in Spain is dead! I felt her cold touch on my back!" - and when that sister IS dead at the moment - what do you call that?'

'Or when the blood of San Gennaro liquefies at the request of the clergy - as all the world knows that it does regularly once a-year, in my native city,' said the

Neapolitan courier after a pause, with a comical look, 'what do you call that?'

'THAT!' cried the German. 'Well, I think I know a name for that.'

'Miracle?' said the Neapolitan, with the same sly face.

The German merely smoked and laughed; and they all smoked and laughed.

'Bah!' said the German, presently. 'I speak of things that really do happen. When I want to see the conjurer, I pay to see a professed one, and have my money's worth. Very strange things do happen without ghosts. Ghosts! Giovanni Baptista, tell your story of the English bride. There's no ghost in that, but something full as strange. Will any man tell me what?'

As there was a silence among them, I glanced around. He whom I took to be Baptista was lighting a fresh cigar. He presently went on to speak. He was a Genoese, as I judged.

'The story of the English bride?' said he. 'Basta! one ought not to call so slight a thing a story. Well, it's all one. But it's true. Observe me well, gentlemen, it's true. That which glitters is not always gold; but what I am going to tell, is true.'

He repeated this more than once.

Ten years ago, I took my credentials to an English gentleman at Long's Hotel, in Bond Street, London, who was about to travel - it might be for one year, it might be for two. He approved of them; likewise of me. He was pleased to make inquiry. The testimony that he received was favourable. He engaged me by the six months, and my entertainment was generous.

He was young, handsome, very happy. He was enamoured of a fair young English lady, with a sufficient fortune, and they were going to be married. It was the wedding-trip, in short, that we were going to take. For three months' rest in the hot weather (it was early summer then) he had hired an old place on the Riviera, at an easy distance from my city, Genoa, on the road to Nice. Did I know that place? Yes; I told him I knew it well. It was an old palace with great gardens. It was a little bare, and it was a little dark and gloomy, being close surrounded by trees; but it was spacious, ancient, grand, and on the seashore. He said it had been so described to him exactly, and he was well pleased that I knew it. For its being a little bare of furniture, all such places were. For its being a little gloomy, he had hired it principally for the gardens, and he and my mistress would pass the summer weather in their shade.

'So all goes well, Baptista?' said he.

'Indubitably, signore; very well.'

We had a travelling chariot for our journey, newly built for us, and in all respects complete. All we had was complete; we wanted for nothing. The marriage took place. They were happy. I was happy, seeing all so bright, being so well situated, going to my own city, teaching my language in the rumble to the maid, la bella Carolina, whose heart was gay with laughter: who was young and rosy.

The time flew. But I observed - listen to this, I pray! (and here the courier dropped his voice) - I observed my mistress sometimes brooding in a manner very strange; in a frightened manner; in an unhappy manner; with a cloudy, uncertain alarm upon her. I think that I began to notice this when I was walking up hills by the carriage side, and master had gone on in front. At any rate, I remember that it impressed itself upon my mind one evening in the South of France, when she called to me to call master back; and when he came back, and walked for a long way, talking encouragingly and affectionately to her, with his hand upon the open window, and hers in it. Now and then, he laughed in a merry way, as if he were bantering her out of something. By-and-by, she laughed, and then all went well again.

It was curious. I asked la bella Carolina, the pretty little one, Was mistress unwell? - No. - Out of spirits? - No. - Fearful of bad roads, or brigands? - No. And what made it more mysterious was, the pretty little one would not look at me in giving answer, but WOULD look at the view.

But, one day she told me the secret.

'If you must know,' said Carolina, 'I find, from what I have overheard, that mistress is haunted.'

'How haunted?'

'By a dream.'

'What dream?'

'By a dream of a face. For three nights before her marriage, she saw a face in a dream - always the same face, and only One.'

'A terrible face?'

'No. The face of a dark, remarkable-looking man, in black, with black hair and a grey moustache - a handsome man except for a reserved and secret air. Not a face she ever saw, or at all like a face she ever saw. Doing nothing in the dream but looking at her fixedly, out of darkness.'

'Does the dream come back?'

'Never. The recollection of it is all her trouble.'

'And why does it trouble her?'

Carolina shook her head.

'That's master's question,' said la bella. 'She don't know. She wonders why, herself. But I heard her tell him, only last night, that if she was to find a picture of that face in our Italian house (which she is afraid she will) she did not know how she could ever bear it.'

Upon my word I was fearful after this (said the Genoese courier) of our coming to the old palazzo, lest some such ill-starred picture should happen to be there. I knew there were many there; and, as we got nearer and nearer to the place, I wished the whole gallery in the crater of Vesuvius. To mend the matter, it was a stormy dismal evening when we, at last, approached that part of the Riviera. It thundered; and the thunder of my city and its environs, rolling among the high hills, is very loud. The lizards ran in and out of the chinks in the broken stone wall of the garden, as if they were frightened; the frogs bubbled and croaked their loudest; the sea-wind moaned, and the wet trees dripped; and the lightning - body of San Lorenzo, how it lightened!

We all know what an old palace in or near Genoa is - how time and the sea air have blotted it - how the drapery painted on the outer walls has peeled off in great flakes of plaster - how the lower windows are darkened with rusty bars of iron - how the courtyard is overgrown with grass - how the outer buildings are dilapidated - how the whole pile seems devoted to ruin. Our palazzo was one of the true kind. It had been shut up close for months. Months? - years! - it had an earthy smell, like a tomb. The scent of the orange trees on the broad back terrace, and of the lemons ripening on the wall, and of some shrubs that grew around a broken fountain, had got into the house somehow, and had never been able to get out again. There was, in every room, an aged smell, grown faint with confinement. It pined in all the cupboards and drawers. In the little rooms of communication between great rooms, it was stifling. If you turned a picture - to come back to the pictures - there it still was, clinging to the wall behind the frame, like a sort of bat.

The lattice-blinds were close shut, all over the house. There were two ugly, grey old women in the house, to take care of it; one of them with a spindle, who stood winding and mumbling in the doorway, and who would as soon have let in the devil as the air. Master, mistress, la bella Carolina, and I, went all through the palazzo. I went first, though I have named myself last, opening the windows and the lattice-blinds, and shaking down on myself splashes of rain, and scraps of mortar, and now and then a dozing mosquito, or a monstrous, fat, blotchy, Genoese spider.

When I had let the evening light into a room, master, mistress, and la bella Carolina, entered. Then, we looked round at all the pictures, and I went forward again into another room. Mistress secretly had great fear of meeting with the likeness of that face - we all had; but there was no such thing. The Madonna and Bambino, San Francisco, San Sebastiano, Venus, Santa Caterina, Angels, Brigands, Friars, Temples at Sunset, Battles, White Horses, Forests, Apostles, Doges, all my old acquaintances many times repeated? - yes. Dark, handsome man in black, reserved and secret, with black hair and grey moustache, looking fixedly at mistress out of darkness? - no.

At last we got through all the rooms and all the pictures, and came out into the gardens. They were pretty well kept, being rented by a gardener, and were large and shady. In one place there was a rustic theatre, open to the sky; the stage a green slope; the coulisses, three entrances upon a side, sweet-smelling leafy screens. Mistress moved her bright eyes, even there, as if she looked to see the face come in upon the scene; but all was well.

'Now, Clara,' master said, in a low voice, 'you see that it is nothing? You are happy.'

Mistress was much encouraged. She soon accustomed herself to that grim palazzo, and would sing, and play the harp, and copy the old pictures, and stroll with master under the green trees and vines all day. She was beautiful. He was happy. He would laugh and say to me, mounting his horse for his morning ride before the heat:

'All goes well, Baptista!'

'Yes, signore, thank God, very well.'

We kept no company. I took la bella to the Duomo and Annunciata, to the Cafe, to the Opera, to the village Festa, to the Public Garden, to the Day Theatre, to the Marionetti. The pretty little one was charmed with all she saw. She learnt Italian - heavens! miraculously! Was mistress quite forgetful of that dream? I asked Carolina sometimes. Nearly, said la bella - almost. It was wearing out.

One day master received a letter, and called me.

'Baptista!'

'Signore!'

'A gentleman who is presented to me will dine here to-day. He is called the Signor Dellombra. Let me dine like a prince.'

It was an odd name. I did not know that name. But, there had been many noblemen and gentlemen pursued by Austria on political suspicions, lately, and some names had changed. Perhaps this was one. Altro! Dellombra was as good a name to me as another.

When the Signor Dellombra came to dinner (said the Genoese courier in the low voice, into which he had subsided once before), I showed him into the reception-room, the great sala of the old palazzo. Master received him with cordiality, and presented him to mistress. As she rose, her face changed, she gave a cry, and fell upon the marble floor.

Then, I turned my head to the Signor Dellombra, and saw that he was dressed in black, and had a reserved and secret air, and was a dark, remarkable-looking man, with black hair and a grey moustache.

Master raised mistress in his arms, and carried her to her own room, where I sent la bella Carolina straight. La bella told me afterwards that mistress was nearly terrified to death, and that she wandered in her mind about her dream, all night.

Master was vexed and anxious - almost angry, and yet full of solicitude. The Signor Dellombra was a courtly gentleman, and spoke with great respect and sympathy of mistress's being so ill. The African wind had been blowing for some days (they had told him at his hotel of the Maltese Cross), and he knew that it was often hurtful. He hoped the beautiful lady would recover soon. He begged permission to retire, and to renew his visit when he should have the happiness of hearing that she was better. Master would not allow of this, and they dined alone.

He withdrew early. Next day he called at the gate, on horse-back, to inquire for mistress. He did so two or three times in that week.

What I observed myself, and what la bella Carolina told me, united to explain to me that master had now set his mind on curing mistress of her fanciful terror. He was all kindness, but he was sensible and firm. He reasoned with her, that to encourage such fancies was to invite melancholy, if not madness. That it rested with herself to be herself. That if she once resisted her strange weakness, so successfully as to receive the Signor Dellombra as an English lady would receive any other guest, it was for ever conquered. To make an end, the signore came again, and mistress received him without marked distress (though with constraint and apprehension still), and the evening passed serenely. Master was so delighted with this change, and so anxious to confirm it, that the Signor Dellombra became a constant guest. He was accomplished in pictures, books, and music; and his society, in any grim palazzo, would have been welcome.

I used to notice, many times, that mistress was not quite recovered. She would cast down her eyes and droop her head, before the Signor Dellombra, or would look at him with a terrified and fascinated glance, as if his presence had some evil influence or power upon her. Turning from her to him, I used to see him in the shaded gardens, or the large half-lighted sala, looking, as I might say, 'fixedly upon her out of darkness.' But, truly, I had not forgotten la bella Carolina's words describing the face in the dream.

After his second visit I heard master say: 'Now, see, my dear Clara, it's over! Dellombra has come and gone, and your apprehension is broken like glass.'

'Will he - will he ever come again?' asked mistress.

'Again? Why, surely, over and over again! Are you cold?' (she shivered).

'No, dear - but - he terrifies me: are you sure that he need come again?'

'The surer for the question, Clara!' replied master, cheerfully.

But, he was very hopeful of her complete recovery now, and grew more and more so every day. She was beautiful. He was happy.

'All goes well, Baptista?' he would say to me again. 'Yes, signore, thank God; very well.'

We were all (said the Genoese courier, constraining himself to speak a little louder), we were all at Rome for the Carnival. I had been out, all day, with a Sicilian, a friend of mine, and a courier, who was there with an English family. As I returned at night to our hotel, I met the little Carolina, who never stirred from home alone, running distractedly along the Corso.

'Carolina! What's the matter?'

'O Baptista! O, for the Lord's sake! where is my mistress?'

'Mistress, Carolina?'

'Gone since morning - told me, when master went out on his day's journey, not to call her, for she was tired with not resting in the night (having been in pain), and would lie in bed until the evening; then get up refreshed. She is gone! - she is gone! Master has come back, broken down the door, and she is gone! My beautiful, my good, my innocent mistress!'

The pretty little one so cried, and raved, and tore herself that I could not have held her, but for her swooning on my arm as if she had been shot. Master came up - in manner, face, or voice, no more the master that I knew, than I was he. He took me (I laid the little one upon her bed in the hotel, and left her with the chamber-women), in a carriage, furiously through the darkness, across the desolate Campagna. When it was day, and we stopped at a miserable post-house, all the horses had been hired twelve hours ago, and sent away in different directions. Mark me! by the Signor Dellombra, who had passed there in a carriage, with a frightened English lady crouching in one corner.

I never heard (said the Genoese courier, drawing a long breath) that she was ever traced beyond that spot. All I know is, that she vanished into infamous oblivion, with the dreaded face beside her that she had seen in her dream.

'What do you call THAT?' said the German courier, triumphantly. 'Ghosts! There are no ghosts THERE! What do you call this, that I am going to tell you? Ghosts! There are no ghosts HERE!'

I took an engagement once (pursued the German courier) with an English gentleman, elderly and a bachelor, to travel through my country, my Fatherland. He was a merchant who traded with my country and knew the language, but who had never been there since he was a boy - as I judge, some sixty years before.

His name was James, and he had a twin-brother John, also a bachelor. Between these brothers there was a great affection. They were in business together, at Goodman's Fields, but they did not live together. Mr. James dwelt in Poland Street, turning out of Oxford Street, London; Mr. John resided by Epping Forest.

Mr. James and I were to start for Germany in about a week. The exact day depended on business. Mr. John came to Poland Street (where I was staying in the house), to pass that week with Mr. James. But, he said to his brother on the second day, 'I don't feel very well, James. There's not much the matter with me; but I think I am a little gouty. I'll go home and put myself under the care of my old housekeeper, who understands my ways. If I get quite better, I'll come back and see you before you go. If I don't feel well enough to resume my visit where I leave it off, why YOU will come and see me before you go.' Mr. James, of course, said he would, and they shook hands - both hands, as they always did - and Mr. John ordered out his old-fashioned chariot and rumbled home.

It was on the second night after that - that is to say, the fourth in the week - when I was awoke out of my sound sleep by Mr. James coming into my bedroom in his flannel-gown, with a lighted candle.

He sat upon the side of my bed, and looking at me, said: 'Wilhelm, I have reason to think I have got some strange illness upon me.'

I then perceived that there was a very unusual expression in his face.

'Wilhelm,' said he, 'I am not afraid or ashamed to tell you what I might be afraid or ashamed to tell another man. You come from a sensible country, where mysterious things are inquired into and are not settled to have been weighed and measured - or to have been unweighable and unmeasurable - or in either case to have been completely disposed of, for all time - ever so many years ago. I have just now seen the phantom of my brother.'

I confess (said the German courier) that it gave me a little tingling of the blood to hear it.

'I have just now seen,' Mr. James repeated, looking full at me, that I might see how collected he was, 'the phantom of my brother John. I was sitting up in bed, unable to sleep, when it came into my room, in a white dress, and regarding me earnestly, passed up to the end of the room, glanced at some papers on my writing-desk, turned, and, still looking earnestly at me as it passed the bed, went out at the door. Now, I am not in the least mad, and am not in the least disposed to invest that phantom with any external existence out of myself. I think it is a warning to me that I am ill; and I think I had better be bled.'

I got out of bed directly (said the German courier) and began to get on my clothes, begging him not to be alarmed, and telling him that I would go myself to the doctor. I was just ready, when we heard a loud knocking and ringing at the street door. My room being an attic at the back, and Mr. James's being the second-floor room in the front, we went down to his room, and put up the window, to see what was the matter.

'Is that Mr. James?' said a man below, falling back to the opposite side of the way to look up.

'It is,' said Mr. James, 'and you are my brother's man, Robert.'

'Yes, Sir. I am sorry to say, Sir, that Mr. John is ill. He is very bad, Sir. It is even feared that he may be lying at the point of death. He wants to see you, Sir. I have a chaise here. Pray come to him. Pray lose no time.'

Mr. James and I looked at one another. 'Wilhelm,' said he, 'this is strange. I wish you to come with me!' I helped him to dress, partly there and partly in the chaise; and no grass grew under the horses' iron shoes between Poland Street and the Forest.

Now, mind! (said the German courier) I went with Mr. James into his brother's room, and I saw and heard myself what follows.

His brother lay upon his bed, at the upper end of a long bed-chamber. His old housekeeper was there, and others were there: I think three others were there, if not four, and they had been with him since early in the afternoon. He was in white, like the figure - necessarily so, because he had his night-dress on. He looked like the figure - necessarily so, because he looked earnestly at his brother when he saw him come into the room.

But, when his brother reached the bed-side, he slowly raised himself in bed, and looking full upon him, said these words: 'JAMES, YOU HAVE SEEN ME BEFORE, TO-NIGHT - AND YOU KNOW IT!'

And so died!

I waited, when the German courier ceased, to hear something said of this strange story. The silence was unbroken. I looked round, and the five couriers were gone: so noiselessly that the ghostly mountain might have absorbed them into its eternal snows. By this time, I was by no means in a mood to sit alone in that awful scene, with the chill air coming solemnly upon me - or, if I may tell the truth, to sit alone anywhere. So I went back into the convent-parlour, and, finding the American gentleman still disposed to relate the biography of the Honourable Ananias Dodger, heard it all out.

Charles Dickens : A Biography

Charles Dickens (1812-1870) is reckoned by many readers and literary critics to be the major English novelist of the Victorian Age. He is remembered today as the author of a series of weighty novels which have been translated into an unlimited number of languages and promoted to the rank of World Classics. The latter include, but are not limited to, *The Adventures of Oliver Twist, A Tale of Two Cities, David Copperfield, A Christmas Carol, Hard Times, Great Expectations* and *The Old Curiosity Shop.*

Birth and Childhood's Hardships

By and large, Charles Dickens's life story is one of somebody who is born and raised in dire straits to become one of the greatest men who have marked human history and thought. It is a perfect example of how the plight of the deprived and the destitute could transform into a precious incentive that pushes them to challenge their circumstances and to unexpectedly excel and shine.

Charles Dickens was born in Portsmouth on February 7th, 1812. His father John Dickens worked as a simple accounting clerk at the Naval Pay Office and the family's pecuniary situation was almost always uneven. When Charles was only two years, the family had to move to London, then later to Chatham. For financial reasons, Charles did not have adequate education. He rather had to leave school at a very young age to work at a polishing and blacking factory. To add insult to injury, Charles's father was imprisoned in 1824 after failing to pay a 40-pound debt.

Charles's experience at the factory played a tremendous role in building the novelist's personality and in deepening his concerns about working children and about the working class in general. Dickens's precocious maturity and the serious responsibilities that he had as a little child left a clear impression on many of his young characters, such as Oliver Twist, David Copperfield and Pip in *Great Expectations*. The hardships that Charles Dickens personally went through made him much interested in defending the poor, in fighting social injustice through exposing its blatant manifestations and in accentuating the importance of having decent work conditions.

Between 1824 and 1827, Dickens's father, who eventually managed to pay his debts, offered Charles the opportunity to attend a private school in North London, the Wellington House Academy. The experience surely enriched the young man's knowledge of the rules of writing and rhetoric and whetted his appetite for 18th-century novels and for the picaresque novels that adorned his father's library. However, during this period, Charles still had to experience another disappointment when his mother refused to spare him the strenuous job at the blacking factory even after the relative improvement of the family's financial situation. The mother's decision had a great psychological impact on young Charles and even influenced his vision of gender roles as he thought that the mother should not be the decision-maker in the family.

Early Publications

Young Charles Dickens occupied numerous jobs and worked hard to learn shorthand. This long and diversified professional experience had a patent impact on his different writings. Indeed, after the blacking factory experience, Dickens first worked as a clerk for attorneys, which allowed him to learn about the legal system and its principles, to become a free-lance reporter for Doctor's Commons Courts in 1829. Later, he even wrote reports for the House of Commons before starting to work for newspapers, magazines and journals.

It was in 1833 that Dickens started writing short stories for a number of literary magazines and journals such as *The Monthly Magazine.* A collection of these texts was later pseudonymously published under the title *Sketches by Boz*. Thanks to Dickens's humor and exceptional writing style, the latter publication was relatively successful, but not as successful as *The Pickwick Papers* whose serial publication sold thousands of copies and raised Dickens to considerable fame. In 1836, he started writing short texts to be published with the humorous illustrations of the famous artist Robert Seymour. These first successes encouraged Dickens to carry on publishing other stories in the form of series. Dickens's next creation was *Oliver Twist* which was published between 1837 and 1839.

It is noteworthy that most of Dickens's novels were published in the form of monthly and weekly chapters which, according to critics and biographers, allowed him to evaluate and adjust his characterizations and plots to meet the expectations of his readership. It was also during this period that Dickens started his long career as a literary magazine editor.

Loves and Marriage

Charles Dickens got married on April 2nd, 1836 to Catherine Thomson Hogarth after one year of engagement. They settled at the famous Furnival's Inn in Holborn, London, before they moved to their home in Bloomsbury. The house was transformed into the Charles Dickens Museum in 1925. Charles and Catherine, who lived there with the first three of their ten children, were joined by Charles's brother Frederick and Catherine's sister Mary. The latter was reported to have had a very special place in Charles's heart. After dying in his own arms in 1837 following a sudden illness, she became a source of inspiration for some of his female characters. After three years of marriage, Dickens's success and rising income made him leave the house for larger and more luxurious estates.

Catherine Hogarth was not Dickens's only love, however. Indeed, biographers report that

Dickens's relation with his wife was sandwiched by two other romantic affairs. First, there was Maria Beadnell, a banker's daughter, with whom Dickens fell in love when he was only eighteen years old. The relationship ended three years later when Maria's parents apparently intervened. The other love story that Dickens went through started in 1857 and pushed him to divorce Catherine the following year. It was when Dickens was having a group of young actresses for the staging of his play *The Frozen Deep* that he fell in love with the actress Ellen Ternan who was 27 years younger than him.

Major Achievements

Charles's first success with *The Pickwick Papers* and *Oliver Twist* only pushed him to devote more time and energy to his writing and editorial activities. After publishing *Nicholas Nickleby* between 1838 and 1839, he started a new project in 1840 that he entitled *Master Humphrey's Clock*. The latter is a collection of stories that share the same frame and have recurring characters. It was among this collection that the two major works *The Old Curiosity Shop* and *Barnaby Rudge* were serially published.

After visiting the United States of America in 1842, Dickens developed a rather negative view of the New World which was mainly depicted in his travelogue *American Notes for General Circulation* and also in his picaresque novel *Martin Chuzzlewit*. The latter included very harsh satire of the republic and strongly denounced its institution of slavery. However, the fury that Dickens caused among some American circles was soon quietened with the publication of *A Christmas Carol* in 1843. The book, which is considered by many as the novelist's finest opus, was celebrated both in England and America.

Two other Christmas books followed respectively in 1834 and 1845. They are *The Chimes* and *The Cricket on the Hearth*. During this period, Dickens also published a new travelogue that he entitled *Pictures from Italy* following his stay in the Mediterranean country. Another Christmas story entitled *The Haunted Man* was published in 1848, which was preceded by *Dombey and Son* (1847) and *The Battle of Life* (1847) and followed by David Copperfield (1849-1850), *Bleak House* (1852-1853) and *Hard Times* (1854).

It was in 1853 that Dickens started organizing public performances in which he presented his literary works. By this time, he also started to collaborate with Wilkie Collins on a number of short stories and plays. *Little Dorrit* started as a monthly serial in 1855 to be finished in 1857. Later, two of Dickens's most valuable works were published: *A Tale of Two Cities* (1859) and *Great Expectations* (1861). They were both published in the weekly periodical, *All the Year Round*, which he founded and edited himself.

Apart from his writings, Dickens's main profitable activity was the public reading of his novels. Along with the money he earned thanks to his successful publications, public readings allowed Dickens to buy his dream house (Gad's Hill Place, Kent), to offer financial help to his parents and brothers and to engage in charitable activities.

Twilight and Death

During the 1860s, Dickens carried on organizing more reading tours. In addition to the many events he had in England, he visited France, the United States, Scotland and Ireland on many an occasion. In 1864, he started his last complete novel, *Our Mutual Friend*. However, by 1865, his health started to waver. This was mainly because of the physical and intellectual exhaustion to which he subjected himself. Furthermore, Dickens was psychologically traumatized in 1865 following a train crash. He was with his beloved Ellen Ternan on their way back from Paris when their train derailed to cause a big number of casualties. Although Dickens was able to collect his courage and managed to help the wounded and comfort them, the picture of the disaster affected him greatly and could never be erased from his mind.

For health reasons, Dickens cancelled many of his programmed readings between 1868 and 1870. On April 22nd, 1869, he had a stroke. The latter was followed by a second stroke on June 8th, 1870, while he was working on his novel *The Mystery of Edwin Drood* which would remain unfinished. The next day, he passed away. Charles Dickens today rests in The Poets' Corner of Westminster Abbey.

www.ingramcontent.com/pod-product-compliance
Lightning Source LLC
LaVergne TN
LVHW010550100826
845148LV00013B/2680

* 9 7 8 1 7 8 0 0 0 6 4 4 4 *